R0202618179

11/2021

W9-AYO-572

Twinkle
and the
Wishing Wand

by Katharine Holabird · illustrated by Cherie Zamazing
in the style of Sarah Warburton

Ready-to-Read

Simon Spotlight
New York   London   Toronto   Sydney   New Delhi

SIMON SPOTLIGHT
An imprint of Simon & Schuster Children's Publishing Division
1230 Avenue of the Americas, New York, New York 10020
This Simon Spotlight edition August 2021
Text copyright © 2021 by Katharine Holabird
Illustrations copyright © 2021 by Sarah Warburton
Illustrations by Cherie Zamazing
For information about special discounts for bulk purchases, please
contact Simon & Schuster Special Sales at 1-866-506-1949 or
business@simonandschuster.com.
Manufactured in the United States of America 0721 LAK
10 9 8 7 6 5 4 3 2 1
Library of Congress Cataloging-in-Publication Data
Names: Holabird, Katharine, author. | Warburton, Sarah, illustrator.
Title: Twinkle and the wishing wand / by Katharine Holabird ; illustrated by Sarah
Warburton.
Description: Simon Spotlight edition. | New York : Simon Spotlight, 2021. | Series:
Twinkle | Audience: Ages 5–7 | Summary: Twinkle and her classmates at the
The Fairy School of Magic and Music are going to the library where all the fairies
select their favorite story and cast a spell to make it come to life.
Identifiers: LCCN 2021003345 (print) | LCCN 2021003346 (ebook) |
ISBN 9781534496712 (hardcover) | ISBN 9781534496705 (paperback) |
ISBN 9781534496729 (ebook)
Subjects: CYAC: Fairies—Fiction. | Magic—Fiction.
Classification: LCC PZ7.H689 Twjt 2021 (print) | LCC PZ7.H689 (ebook) |
DDC [E]—dc23
LC record available at https://lccn.loc.gov/2021003345
LC ebook record available at https://lccn.loc.gov/2021003346

Twinkle was a pink fairy.
When she was excited,
her wings glowed!

Today Twinkle's wings
were glowing very brightly.
The fairies at The Fairy School
of Magic and Music were
going to one of Twinkle's favorite
places—the library!

"Tra-la-la! Foo-fee-fee!
I can't wait to sit and read!"
Twinkle sang.

"When we get to the library,"
Miss Flutterbee said,
"please pick out a book.

Then please practice
your storytime spells!"

"Watch me," Miss Flutterbee said,
waving her wand.
"Abracadabra! Fiddle-fee-fee!
Open this book and read it to me!"

Miss Flutterbee's book opened.
Twinkle could hear music
coming from it!
Then a sweet, soft voice
began to read the words aloud.

Twinkle and the fairies flew
to the library.
The librarian was so happy
to see them.
"Welcome, fairies.
Let me know if I can help you
find a book
for your storytime spell."

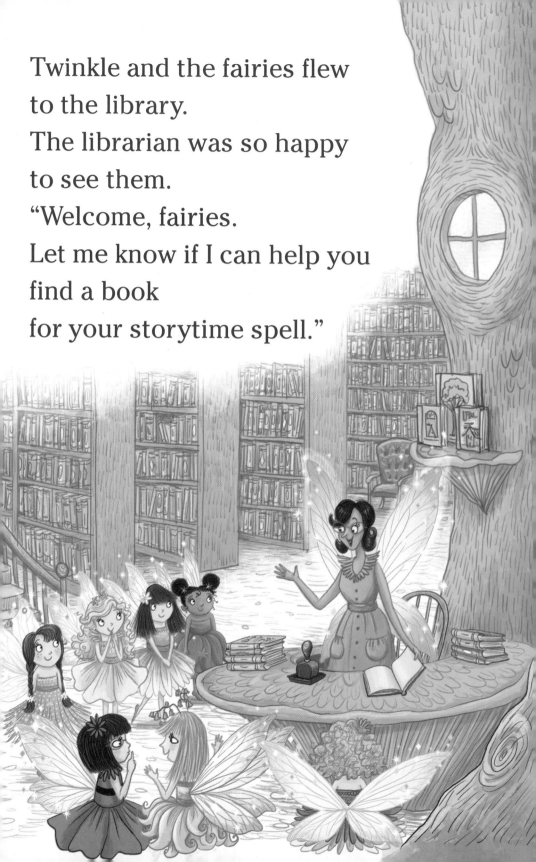

Twinkle and her best friends,
Lulu and Pippa, flew off
to explore the shelves of books.

Twinkle rounded a corner
and found one of her favorite books,
Princess Sparkles Saves the Castle!

Twinkle hugged the book tightly.
Then her wings glowed
extra brightly!
She couldn't wait to try
the storytime spell.

Twinkle picked a cozy spot and opened the book.
As Twinkle flipped through the pages, she started wishing she could meet Princess Sparkles in real life.

Twinkle pulled out her wand
and whispered a different spell
than the one Miss Flutterbee gave
the class earlier.

"Abracadabra! Tweedle-dee-dee!
Let this book come to life for me!"

Suddenly, dragons, unicorns, and trolls started pouring out of the book!
"Oh no!" Twinkle said.
Twinkle tried another spell.

"Abracadabra! Shoodle-shee-shook!
Put everyone back,
and close this book!"

But nothing happened.
And the dragons, unicorns, and trolls
were making lots of noise
in the library.

"Shh!" Twinkle heard the librarian say.
Twinkle didn't know what to do.
She took a deep breath
and then tried another spell
she knew would work.

"Abracadabra! Fiddle-dee-doo!
I need my friends, Pippa and Lulu!"

Pippa and Lulu flew over
with their wands.

"Don't worry, Twinks," Lulu said.
"We're here to help!" Pippa said,
putting her arm around her friend.

Pippa flew around the library.
The dragons started following her.

Lulu found the unicorns and trolls
and led them back to Twinkle's book.

Twinkle looked at the book
and grabbed her wand.
She needed someone else's help.
"Abracadabra! Skiddle-dee-doo!
I need Princess Sparkles, too!"

Just then Princess Sparkles appeared, waving her own wand.

She turned the dragons
into butterflies.
She turned the trolls into flowers.

Princess Sparkles jumped
onto the back of one of the unicorns
and led everyone into the book.

Twinkle could not believe it.
Princess Sparkles saved her castle
from the dragons and trolls,
and helped save the library too!

"Thank you, Princess Sparkles,"
Twinkle said.
From inside the book,
Princess Sparkles waved.
Twinkle looked up.
"Thank you, Pippa and Lulu."

"We will always be here to
help our friend," Pippa said.

Then Twinkle and her friends closed
the book and made their last wishing
spell together.

"Abracadabra! Fiddle-fee-fee!
Open this book and read it to me!"

Twinkle, Pippa, and Lulu
sat in some comfy chairs
and listened to the story of
their favorite hero together.
It was a wonderful day
spent reading with friends!